# THE TREK

Ann Jonas

Greenwillow Books, New York

For Susan,
and of course,
Don, Nina + Amy



Printed in Hong Kong
by South China Printing Co.
First Edition 10 9 8 7 6 5 4 3 2 1

Library of Congress
Cataloging in Publication Data
Jonas, Ann. The trek.
Summary: A child describes her trip through a jungle and across a desert—right on the way to school.
1. Children's stories, American.
[1. Jungles—Fiction.
2. Deserts—Fiction.
3. Imagination—Fiction] I. Title.
PZ7.J664Tr 1985 [E] 84-25962
ISBN 0-688-04799-8
ISBN 0-688-04800-5 (lib. bdg.)

My mother
doesn't walk me
to school anymore.

But she doesn't know
we live on the edge
of a jungle.

She doesn't even see
what's right outside our door!

There are creatures everywhere.
But they can't hide from me.

BUS
STOP

Some of my animals are dangerous
and it's only my amazing skill
that saves me day after day.

Look at that!
The waterhole is really
crowded today.

What will they do when this herd
goes down to drink?

Here's my helper, right on time.
Now we can cross
the desert together.

Those animals won't see us
if we stay behind the sand dunes.
Be very quiet.

That woman doesn't know
about the animals.
If she did, she'd be scared.

We missed the boat!
Now we'll have to swim
across the river.

COIN
OPERATED

Be careful! This jungle is full of animals.

VEGETABLES
EGGPLANT

The trading post at last!
No time to stop!

COFFEE SHOPPE

We're almost there,
only the mountain
to climb.

We made it!

SOME ANIMALS WE KNOW
MOOSE
ALLIGATOR
PORCUPINE
ALPACA
TURKEY
SPIDER
PANGOLIN
WARTHOG
ZEBRA
MONKEY
LIZARD
BONGO
CAMEL
PEACOCK
YAK
VULTURE
SEA LION
LEOPARD

MORE ANIMALS WE KNOW
OSTRICH
HIPPOPOTAMUS
KOALA
WATER BUFFALO
PIG
PYTHON
GORILLA
SWAN
RHINOCEROS
SHEEP
GIRAFFE
CASSOWARY
TURTLE
ELEPHANT
TIGER
ORANGUTAN
FISH
ORYX